Helen Orme taught for many years before giving up teaching to write full-time. At the last count she had written over 70 books.

She writes both fiction and non-fiction, but at present is concentrating on fiction for older readers.

Helen also runs writing workshops for children and courses for teachers in both primary and secondary schools.

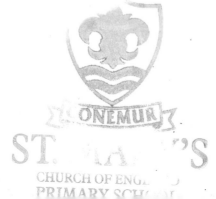

ONEMUR

ST. S

CHURCH OF ENG
PRIMARY SCH

How many have you read?

Two years on:

Leave Her Alone

 Helen Orme

Ransom

Leave Her Alone

by Helen Orme
Illustrated by Chris Askham

Published by Ransom Publishing Ltd.
Radley House, 8 St. Cross Road, Winchester, Hampshire
SO23 9HX, UK
www.ransom.co.uk

ISBN   978 184167 742 2

First published in 2011
Copyright © 2011 Ransom Publishing Ltd.

Illustrations copyright © 2011 Chris Askham

Meet the Sisters ...

Siti and her friends are really close. So close she calls them her Sisters. They've been mates for ever, and most of the time they are closer than her real family.

Siti is the leader – the one who always knows what to do – but Kelly, Lu, Donna and Rachel have their own lives to lead as well.

Still, there's no one you can talk to, no one you can rely on, like your best mates. Right?

1

The new car

It all started when Lu's dad got a new car.

'What does he want another new car for?' asked Siti.

'You know my dad.' Lu shrugged her shoulders.

'My mum calls cars like that *boys' toys*,' said Kelly.

'Yeah, but,' said Rachel 'It is cool.'

Siti wasn't that interested in cars. Rachel was though.

'Wow!' she said. 'A Merc! I wish my mum would get something better.'

Kelly laughed. She'd been in Rachel's mum's car.

'Anything would be better than your mum's car,' she said.

Lu's dad wanted to show off the car. He came to pick up Lu after school.

'Please Dad,' said Lu. 'Don't bother.'

'No bother,' said her dad. 'I'll give the others lifts too.'

Lu was embarrassed. 'I wish he wouldn't do it,' she told Siti. 'Sometimes he treats me as if I'm ten!'

'Don't worry,' said Siti. 'We'll all come. If we all talk together, very loudly, your dad will soon get fed up with it.'

9

In the car they tried Siti's plan, but it didn't work. Lu's dad just ignored them. He knew that Rachel was keen on cars and he spent the whole time telling her about it.

He was so pleased with the car he insisted on coming to meet them the next day as well. Worst of all, he parked right outside the school gates.

2

Who does she think she is?

It wouldn't have been so bad if it hadn't been for Kathryn and her friends. Kathryn was stuck up. Her family had lots of money and they lived in a big house. Her dad had just bought a new hybrid car.

She saw the Sisters getting into Mr Clarke's car. She turned to Sarah and Laura.

'Look at them,' she said loudly. 'My dad would never buy that. He cares about the environment.'

'My mum thinks that cars like that are too flash,' agreed Sarah.

Mr Clarke didn't hear them but Lu did. So did Siti.

'Ignore them,' said Siti. 'They'll soon get tired of it.'

3

Saying things

Siti's advice was usually good, but this time she was wrong. They didn't get tired of it.

Kathryn began to get really nasty. She made comments about Lu's dad.

'What a prat,' she said. 'No one buys cars like that now.'

Then they started saying things about her mum.

'Her mum worked in a Chinese takeaway,' said Sarah.

'Do you eat Chinese all the time at home?' sneered Laura.

'Shut up,' said Siti. 'There's nothing wrong with working in a takeaway.'

'Maybe not to you,' said Kathryn. 'But then your sort don't understand how things work, do you?'

'I understand what you are,' said Siti. She was getting really angry now. 'You are just a

nasty racist. If it doesn't stop I'm going to tell my dad.'

'You do that and you'll be sorry!'

Kathryn went off. Sarah and Laura followed her, laughing.

'I'm going to see my dad now,' said Siti.

Her dad was a deputy head at their school.

'Don't,' begged Lu. 'It'll only make things worse. You heard what they said.'

4

A real bully

Siti's threat did help. Kathryn, Sarah and Laura backed off a bit.

They stopped saying things when the Sisters were around. But they still made Lu feel bad.

Kathryn got a menu from a Chinese takeaway. She copied some of the Chinese from the menu onto her pencil case. She would swing the case round by its strap to make her friends laugh.

The Sisters did what they could.

'She's just being spiteful,' said Kelly. 'She thinks she's better than everyone else.'

'She's a real bully,' said Donna. 'I hate her.'

'We'll make sure we're together all the time,' said Siti. 'She's scared that I will tell my dad if she goes on at you too much.'

But they couldn't be together all the time. They were in different groups for some lessons.

When Lu was by herself Kathryn was much, much nastier. She came up behind Lu

and whispered horrible things in her ear. The things she said about Lu's mum made Lu want to cry.

It got so bad that Lu even stopped telling the Sisters.

She didn't want Siti talking to her dad. It would just make everything worse.

5

We've got to do something

Lu was heading for the dining hall. She was by herself.

Kathryn ran up behind her. She grabbed Lu's arm and twisted hard. Lu cried out. Before she could stop herself she hit Kathryn.

Kathryn screamed, really loudly.

'I'm sorry, I didn't mean it.' Lu was nearly crying.

Miss Drake rushed out of the dining hall.

'Whatever is going on?' she asked.
'Kathryn, stop that noise. Lu, what did you do?'

'She slapped me,' said Kathryn.

Lu didn't know what to say.

'Come with me,' said Ms Drake. 'We're going to your Head of Year. She can sort you out!'

'What did you tell her?' Donna asked later.

'Nothing.'

'Why not? You should have told her what was going on.' That was Siti, of course.

'There's no point. She's bad enough anyway. Think what she'll be like if I tell.'

'What's going to happen?' asked Kelly.

'I've got to stay after school tomorrow and write a letter of apology.'

Siti was furious. '*You've* got to apologise to *her*?'

'We've got to do something,' said Donna. 'She's got to be stopped.'

Siti tried to talk to her dad.

'You know I can't tell you anything,' he said.

'Yes, but ...' said Siti. 'It's not fair!'

'Then talk to your form tutor, or head of year,' said Mr Musa. 'Tell them everything you've told me. Better still, get Lu to talk to them.'

But Lu would not tell anybody.

'What about your mum?' said Kelly.

'I can't tell her. You know the sorts of things Kathryn's been saying. It would really upset mum. There's nothing I can do. There's nothing anyone can do.'

6

Real trouble

But Mr Musa was worried. He talked to the other teachers.

'Keep an eye on Lu please,' he asked. 'We can't let this go on.'

Kathryn thought she was safe. It was Lu who had got into trouble, not her. She began to say nasty things again.

But she wasn't as clever as she thought. They were in maths. Kathryn was sitting behind Lu. She kept kicking the back of Lu's chair. Miss Harper was watching. She walked to the back of the class.

As she went past Kathryn and Lu she heard what Kathryn was saying.

She asked them to stay behind at the end of the lesson.

'I heard everything you said to Lu,' she told Kathryn. 'You are in real trouble.'

She took both girls back to their year head, Mrs Barnes.

Mrs Barnes talked to Lu first. Lu told her everything.

'Why didn't you tell me before?' she asked.

'I was frightened,' said Lu. 'I didn't know what Kathryn would do.'

'Don't worry,' said Mrs Barnes. 'It's going to end – now!'

Kathryn was suspended for the rest of the week.

Mr Lester explained to Lu.

'Before Kathryn comes back she will come into school with her parents. You, and your parents, will be able to talk to her as well.'

Lu wasn't looking forward to it.

'I bet her mum and dad are just like her,' she said to the Sisters.

7

Like sisters

The meeting was fixed for Monday afternoon. Lu worried all morning.

Her mum and dad arrived. Lu took them to Mrs Barnes' office and knocked on the door.

Kathryn and her mum and dad were already there. Kathryn did not look happy.

Nor did Mr and Mrs Mason.

But Lu was in for a shock. When her mum and dad walked in, Mrs Mason suddenly smiled and jumped up.

'Lin! I haven't seen you for years!' She went over to Lu's mum and took her hand.

'Vicky! I didn't even know you still lived round here!'

Kathryn stared at them, horrified.

Mrs Barnes coughed. 'I think we should get on with this,' she said firmly.

She looked hard at Kathryn. 'I think you have something to say to Lu.'

Kathryn looked at her dad. He nodded.

'Go on then.'

'I'm sorry,' she said, not really looking at Lu. 'I didn't really mean those things I said. It was just a joke.'

'A joke that went too far,' said Mrs Barnes. 'We will be watching you Kathryn. Don't let it happen again.'

Outside, the two mums had big smiles on their faces.

'How come you know each other?' asked Lu.

'We went to school together. Vicky was my best friend.'

'We were like sisters!' said Mrs Mason. 'We spent all our time together.'

'Yes,' added Lu's mum. 'Vicky used to work with me at weekends and holidays in the restaurant.'

'That was such fun,' said Mrs Hammond. 'No one ever cooked such good Chinese food as your mum.'

'I wish I'd seen Kathryn's face when her mum said that,' laughed Siti.

Lu was telling the Sisters all about it at hometime.

'She went bright red,' said Lu. 'She didn't know what to say!'

Lu's mum was pleased to meet up with her old friend again. Lu's dad got on well with Mr Mason too.

So well that it wasn't long before he turned up at school with another new car.

'I've gone green,' he told Rachel. 'I've sold the Merc and got this instead.'

It was a brand new hybrid!